Please write to
Hsiao Publishing
8553 N. Beach St. PMB 379, Fort Worth, TX 76244

ISBN 978-0-9993079-5-3 (Paperback Edition)
Library of Congress Control Number: 2019909210

ISBN 978-0-9993079-6-0 (Ebook Edition)

Special thanks to Gravit Designer

It's a WonderPho Christmas

by Y.T. Tran

HSIAO

Lillian has been dreaming of this Christmas since last Christmas.

In her dreams, she sees everything she wants.

Finally, it's three days until Christmas.
It's very cold outside.

Lillian doesn't want to stay in her warm and toasty house.

She wants to go Christmas shopping with Dad at the mall.

She puts on her coat, hat, and mittens.
She's ready to go.

Lillian shows Dad a long list for Christmas.
"I need a lot of new things," says Lillian.

Dad says he is buying presents for other people, too. He only has enough money to buy one thing on her list.

Telescope
Microscope
Easel
Canvas
Paint
New Desk
New Chair
Roald Dahl Books!!!

"Maybe Mom, Grandfather, Grandmother, Aunt and Uncle can each give me one thing on my list. Then, I'll have everything," says Lillian.

On the way to the mall, Dad gives money to a man on the street. The man is shaking. He doesn't have a coat, hat, or mittens. Lillian asks Dad why the man is standing in the cold. Dad says that he may not have a place to stay.

"Then where does he sleep?"
asks Lillian.

"One of the shelters, if they
have space," says Dad.

Lillian is worried. What if the
shelters don't have space?

ANYTHING
HELPS!
THANK YOU!

It is very warm and toasty inside the mall. Lillian takes off her coat, hat, and mittens.

She helps Dad get presents for everyone in the family. They can't find anything on her list. She is not happy.

"Let's have pho for lunch," says Dad. "A hot bowl of noodles is wonderful on a cold day. That will cheer us up."

Lillian puts bean sprouts and basil in her soup of rice noodles and meatballs. She adds one tiny piece of chili pepper. A few drops of lime juice and fish sauce go in, too.

"My pho looks like a garden. It smells so fresh." Lillian puts her face close to the steaming noodles. She tastes her soup. "It's a little salty, a little sour, a little spicy, and a lot of yummy."

When Lillian is done eating, her tummy is full and warm. The pho has cheered her up. And she has an idea.

Lillian says, "What if the man on the street only has enough money to buy one thing? If he buys food, he won't have money for a coat, hat, or mittens. He won't have money to sleep in a hotel.

"So, what if, instead of buying something for me, you buy him pho? And Mom, Grandfather, Grandmother, Aunt and Uncle each buys him something, too. I can wait till next Christmas for the things I want. The man can't wait till next Christmas to eat and get warm."

Dad agrees.

Lillian and Dad go to the man. They tell him to go inside the mall and have pho. The man says, "Thank you," over and over.

Lillian doesn't know why, but she is very happy.

Video Chat: On

That night, Lillian tells her family what she wants them to do. They all like her idea very much.

The next day, the house is still warm and toasty. Lillian draws with her old crayons.

She plays with her old toys. She uses her old binoculars and magnifying glass. She cuddles with her old blanket. She reads her favorite book again.

She doesn't need anything new after all.

It's Christmas Eve. Lillian and Dad go back to find the man on the street. They want to give him the coat, hat, mittens, and a gift card for hotel.

THE MALL

SHOP

DINE

PLAY

They can't find him. Lillian is a little sad.
Dad says, "Let's go and have pho again."

They go inside the mall. Lillian sees a line of people. They are donating warm clothes and sleeping bags.

A man and a woman come to Lillian and Dad. The man is the person they are looking for.

"Here you are," Lillian says. "We have gifts for you."

The man says, "You are very kind. You asked your dad to use money for your Christmas present to buy pho for me. The money was enough to buy ten bowls of pho. So, I brought my friends because they were hungry, too."

The woman is the boss of the mall. She says other customers want to help, too. They buy more food for the man and his friends. She has a space in the mall for them to stay for the winter.

Other malls are doing the same thing now. People all over the city are giving money and warm things. They will help the homeless who can't go to shelters.

Dad tells Lillian, "Your small gift became a very big gift."

Later that night, Lillian goes to sleep thinking that helping others is the best Christmas gift of all. She has never felt happier.

And she dreams, next year, instead of the things on her list this year, she will ask her father to give somebody pho for Christmas again.

Why do you think Lillian is so happy at the end of the story even though she doesn't get anything on her list?

Write down 3 ideas to help someone have a wonderful Christmas:

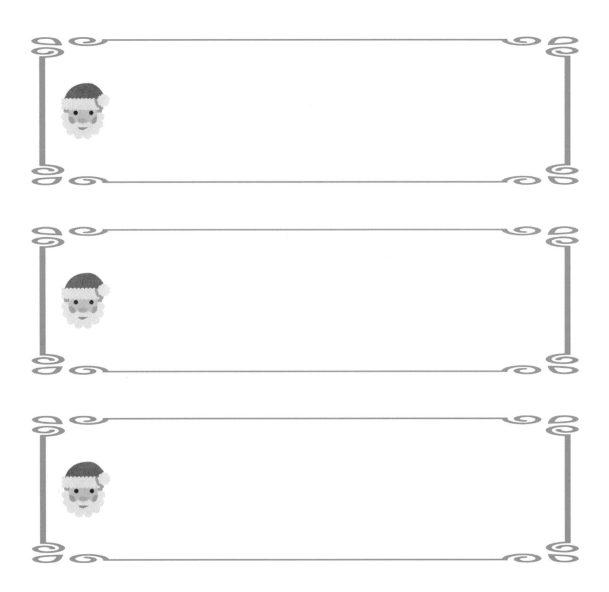

Easy Christmas Pho Recipe for Kids with Help from Their Loving Adults

Pho is the Vietnamese name for long, flat rice noodles, and you can make pho noodle soup any way you like. You can make pho bo, which is pho with beef, or pho ga, which is pho with chicken. Pho chay is pho with vegetables only. You can have pho anytime. In Vietnam, you can see pho being sold on the street and people sitting on low stools to eat pho for breakfast.

Here is a simple way to make pho that smells and tastes very close to what you find in Vietnam.

Ingredients:

1) One package of Banh Pho, otherwise known as rice sticks, or flat rice noodles. You can use Pad Thai noodles, too.

2) 64 oz of water (or 2 of 32 oz chicken, beef, or vegetable broth from the store)

3) Cooked mini chicken meatballs (or other type of meatballs, even vegetarian ones)

4) One green vegetable, like broccoli florets, lightly steamed or boiled

5) One red vegetable, like cherry tomatoes

6) Mix spices: 1 tsp five-spice powder* + 1 tsp ginger powder + 1 tsp onion powder + 1 tsp salt

Optional: Lime or lemon wedges, basil (either Thai or Italian), bean sprouts, fish sauce, and other condiments as desired.

* Five-spice powder should have cinnamon, cloves, fennel, star anise, and Szechwan peppercorns.

Steps:

1) Cook banh pho according to package instructions. Usually, you soak noodles in cold or room temperature water for 30 minutes and then you boil them for 2-5 minutes, depending on how soft you like them. Drain water and divide noodles into bowls. (4-8 bowls, depending on how hungry each person is.)

2) Add cooked broccoli florets and cherry tomatoes to the bowls.

3) In a separate pot, bring 64 oz of water (or broth) to boil.

4) Add in the spice mix.

5) Add in the cooked meatballs.

6) Turn off heat after 1 minute.

7) Ladle soup with meatballs into the bowls of noodles. And there you have it!

Christmas Pho.

(Add the optional items if you wish.)

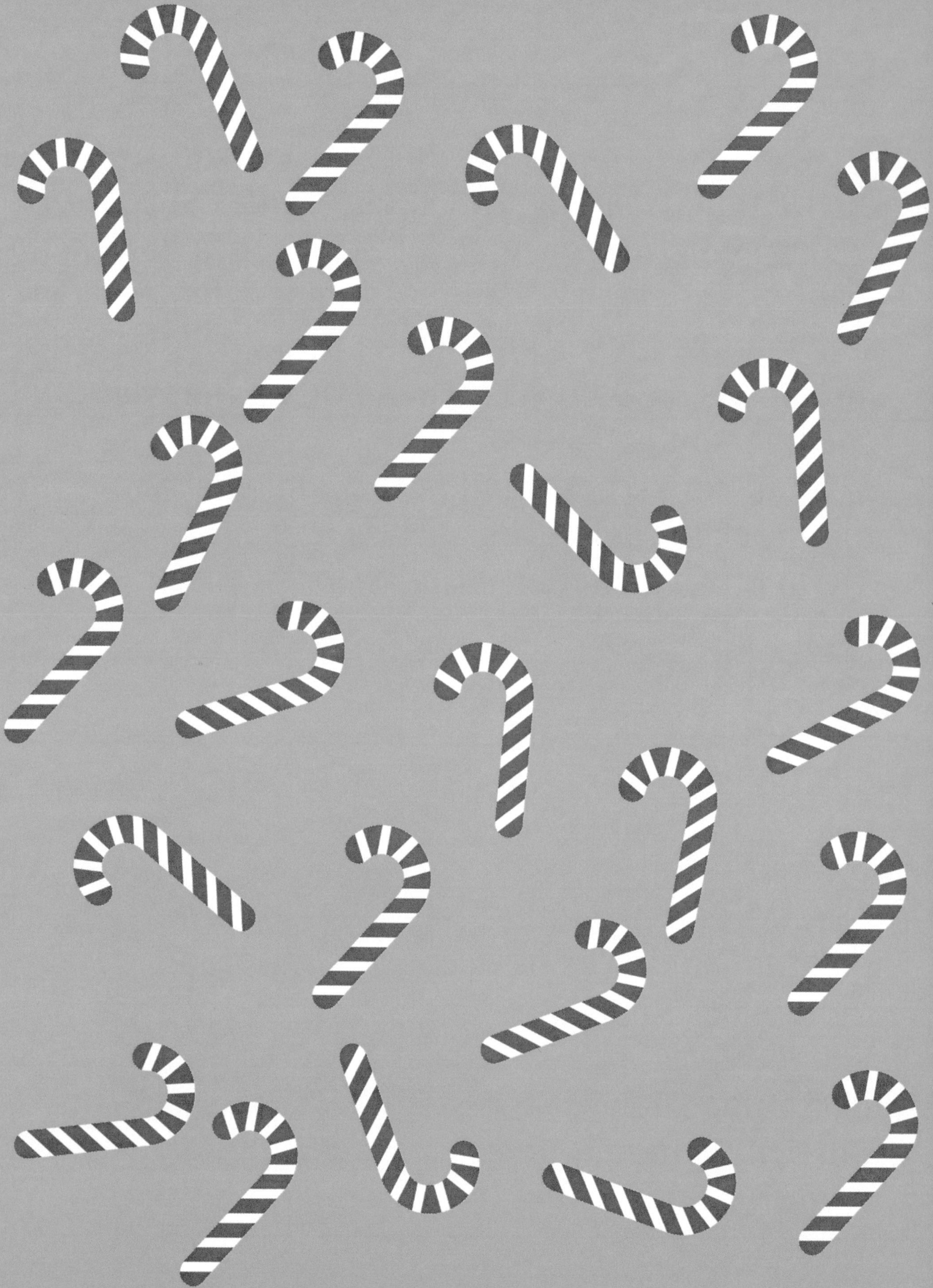

Made in the USA
Coppell, TX
10 November 2019